First there was *Spoon*. Then came *Chopsticks*. And now the last . . .

STRAW

written by

Amy Krouse Rosenthal

illustrated by

Scott Magoon

DISNEP · HYPERION
Los Angeles   New York

First Edition, February 2020
10 9 8 7 6 5 4 3 2 1
FAC-029191-19354
Printed in Malaysia

This book is set in Filosofia OT, Proxima Nova Condensed/Fontspring
Designed by Mary Claire Cruz
The illustrations in this book were created using digital tools.

Library of Congress Cataloging-in-Publication Control Number: 2018056846
ISBN 978-1-4847-4955-5
Reinforced binding
Visit www.DisneyBooks.com

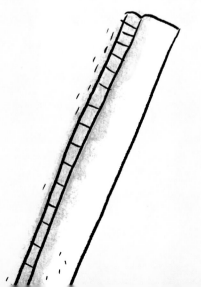

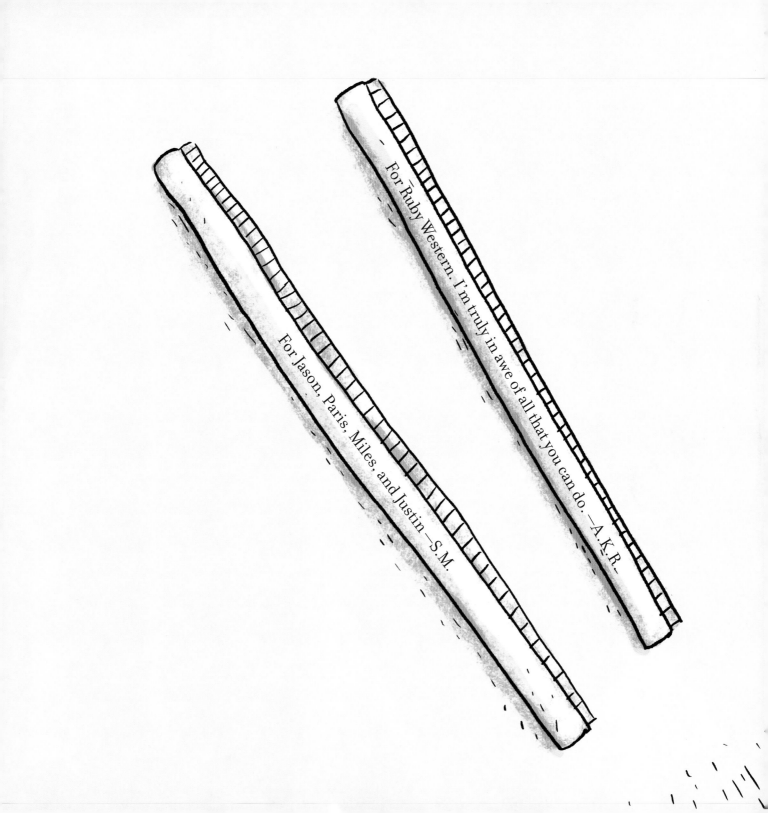

For Ruby Western. I'm truly in awe of all that you can do. —A.K.R.

For Jason, Paris, Miles, and Justin —S.M.

This

is Straw's story.

Straw has a great big family of all stripes and colors.

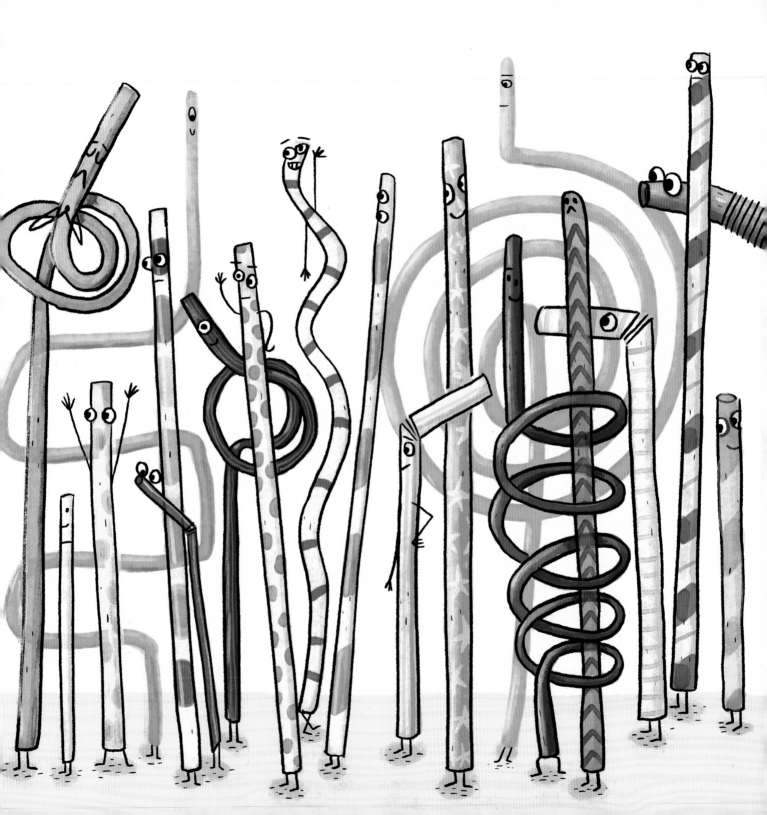

Straw has a great bunch of friends.

And Straw has a great thirst for being first.

"Done!"

As in, Straw REALLY likes to be first.

It was just Straw's way.

Straw probably would have kept racing along, but one day, something unusual happened.

Something that did not feel good—not even one little bit.

"Brain Freeze!"

Every fast slurp only made it worse.

While his
head throbbed,

his heart

sank.

Meanwhile, over in the corner,
one of his glassmates could see that
Straw was feeling low.

"Hi, Straw.
Do you wanna play?!"

"I dunno. . . ."

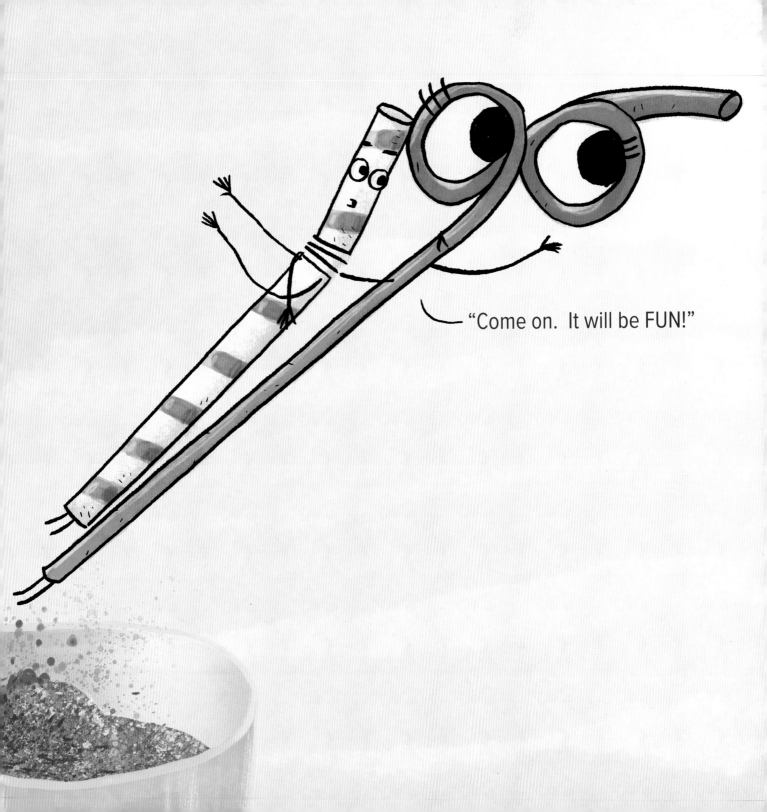

"Come on. It will be FUN!"

She started blowing bubbles.

Beautiful glistening bubbles
that floated up

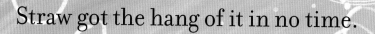

Straw got the hang of it in no time.

He was all bubbly and giggly.

That is, until . . .

"Not everything's a race, Straw. Some things are meant to be savored.

I mean, I know I take the long way and meander more than most, but . . ."

"Sometimes you just gotta stop and smell the milk shake!"

Straw hadn't thought of it that way before.

That night, after bedtime stories, Straw couldn't stop talking about all the things he had seen that day.

"The most reddest strawberry!"

"Swirly swirls in the whipped cream!"

He lay in bed.

His mind
was racing.

There's no need to drink it all in tonight, he remembered.

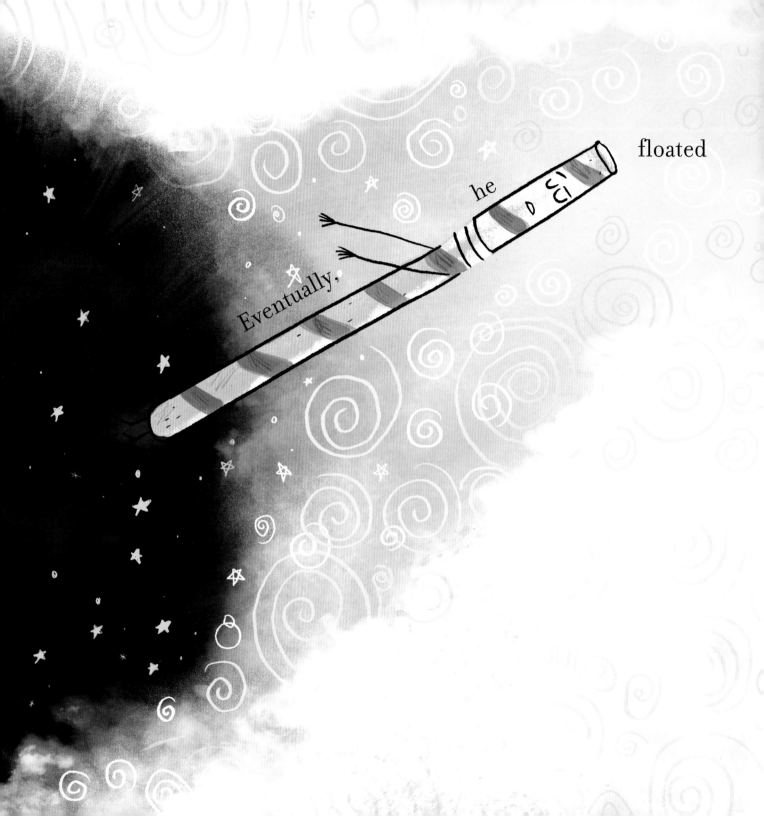

Eventually, he floated

off   to

sleep.

And what can I tell you about Straw now?

Well, sometimes he still wants to be first.
But *most* of the time,
    Straw wants to make the good things *last*.